Where Three Oceans Meet

BY
RAJANI LAROCCA

ILLUSTRATED BY
ARCHANA SREENIVASAN

Abrams Books for Young Readers

New York

We decide to travel to the very tip
of India, where three oceans meet.

Pati, Mommy, and me.

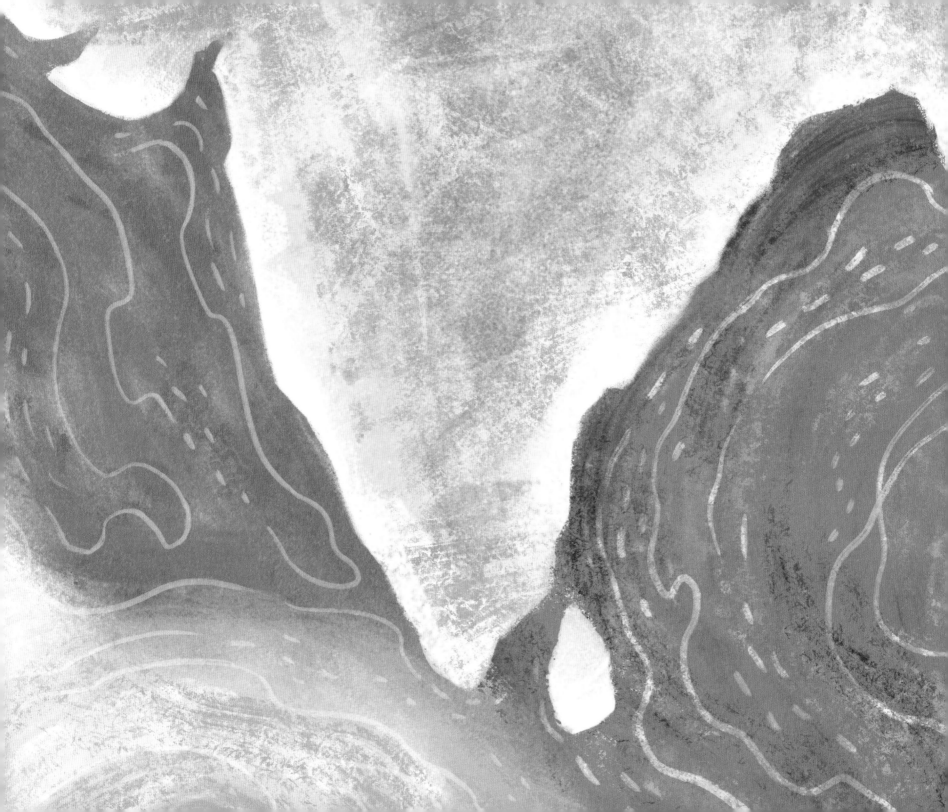

"I want to go to temples," says Pati.

"I want to visit friends," says Mommy.

I say, "I want to see what's at the end of the earth!"

"Yes, Sejal," they say. "We'll see it together."

And so we plan our trip.

Pati and Mommy
speak Tamil.

Mommy and I
speak English.

Pati and I speak a mishmash of Tamil and English and Kannada. When we are confused, we act things out.

"Let's go by car," says Pati.

"And by train," says Mommy.

I ask, "Can we take a boat?"

"Yes, Sejal," they say. "We'll take one together."

Mommy is tallest, but not by much.
I am shortest. But maybe not for long.

We pack our clothes.

Pati's saris, made of heavy silk,
are nine yards long and cover her
from neck to ankle.

Mommy's saris are six yards long
and flutter with bright colors.

I bring T-shirts and jeans, and langas and blouses for dressing up. I pack my special sandals for the end of the earth. I wonder what we'll find there.

We ride in a car on noisy streets.
Pati tells me jokes between the
driver's beeps of the horn.

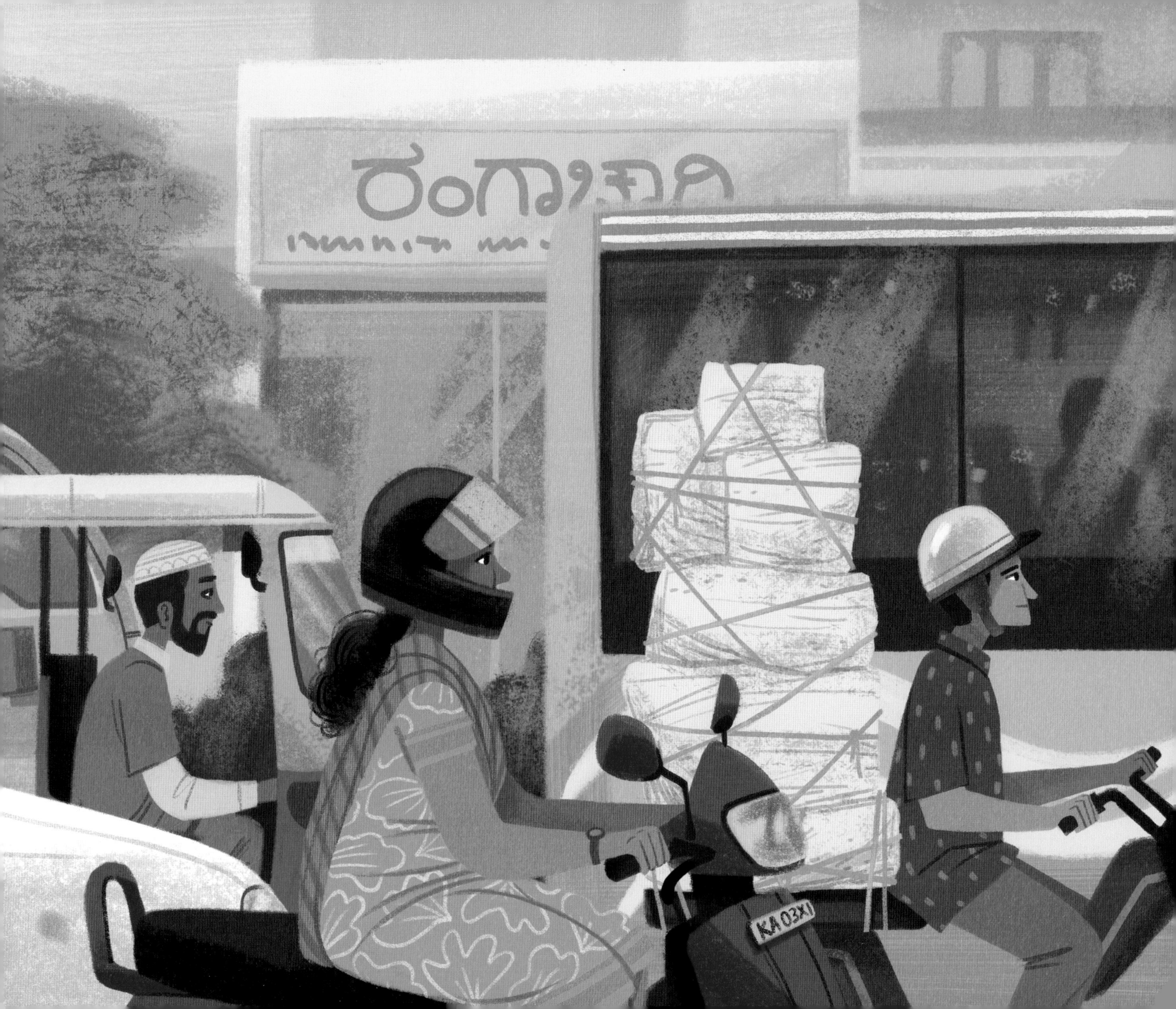
KA 03X1

In Chennai, we share a crisp paper
dosa as big as the table.

Pati eats it with potatoes and onions.

Mommy adds spicy lemon pickle.

I like mine with sugar and ghee.

We doze on a train as the countryside flashes by.
Mommy points out cows and farmers' carts.

In Coimbatore,
we visit friends.

Pati drinks tea with
the grandparents.

Mommy and her friend can't stop giggling.

I play running and catching, which is exactly like tag.

We take a long, slow boat ride down a winding river. I love it, but I want to go faster.

I ask, "When will we reach the end of the earth?"

"Soon, Sejal," they say. "We'll reach it together."

In the hot afternoon, we sip water
straight from tender green coconuts
with their tops sliced off.

In the cool evening, we shop for bright dresses and jingling bangles.

We munch on boiled peanuts sold right on the street.

One day I get the sniffles, and we stay
in our hotel room with the fan droning.

Pati feeds me a sweet musambi,
piece by piece, each section peeled.

I rest my head in Mommy's lap.

And as my eyes close, I hear them talk.

About how Pati lost her
mother when she was
smaller than me.

How Mommy's raising me
in a place so far from here.

How we miss each other as days
flow into months and years.

I still want to see the end of the earth.
But I open my eyes and say,
"I never want this trip to end."

Pati and Mommy hold me tight.

When I feel better,
Mommy brushes my hair,
then brushes her own
that coils down her
back in waves.

She shows me how to take three
sections and twist them, over and
under, over and under again and
again, into a braid that is stronger
than any piece alone.

In Madurai, we visit the temple and see the Goddess.

We pray for good luck, and strength for girls and women.

And when we reach the very tip of India,
we stand together at Kanyakumari,
the place where three oceans meet.

Pati, Mommy, and me.
One who lives in India,
one who moved to America,
one who belongs to both.

We gaze at the water
where blue and green and gray connect.
And I find what's at the end of the earth.

Three entwined as one,
stronger than any alone.

Author's Note

This story was inspired by a trip my family and I took through South India when I was a child.

When I was a baby, my parents and I immigrated to the United States, but our minds were never far from our loved ones in India. Every few years, we traveled back to spend the whole summer with our relatives. My mom and I would go first and stay for eight to nine weeks, and my dad would join us for the last two or three.

My extended family lives in the wonderful city of Bangalore, which is filled with beautiful gardens and parks, lots of terrific food, and incredible music and art. One year, a few of us took a meandering trip from Bangalore all the way through South India.

This is a work of fiction, but my family, like Sejal's, went to temples and visited friends, ate delicious meals, and experienced nature in its glory. We ended up at Kanyakumari, at the very southern tip of the Indian subcontinent, where people say three oceans meet. And when I looked out into the boundless water, I could see three different colors coming together and swirling into one.

It's a curious thing about road trips: We tend to think about where we begin and end and the exciting sights along the way, but ultimately, it's the little moments that are most precious. When I look back on that trip now, I think of all the minutes and hours and days I spent with my family, how close I felt to them, and how our love has never faded, despite distance and time.

Illustrator's Note

When I read the manuscript for *Where Three Oceans Meet*, I was instantly excited. For starters, I was born in Bangalore—the city where Sejal and her family start on their journey—and continue to live here. Sadly, though, Bangalore's claim of being a garden city is seriously threatened at this time, as we are rapidly losing green spaces to meet the needs of a growing population.

I was born into a Tamil-speaking family, but we also speak Kannada and English at home, just like Sejal and her family do! And working on this book sent me on a nostalgic trip back to my own childhood. I was reminded of my grandmothers—whom I also called "Paati," the Tamil word for *Grandma*—who often wore nine-yard saris and were very much interested in visiting temples. The illustrations of Sejal's Pati are based on my maternal grandmother. In fact, some of the saris Sejal's grandmother wears are replicas of those my maternal grandmother wore.

I've tried to weave into the illustrations lots of little details that hold meaning and nostalgic value to me. For example: the ammikallu, or manual stone grinder, that Sejal's mother is using in the kitchen; the ubiquitous "Godrej" steel almirah that stands open in Pati's room as they pack for their trip; the tulsi katte at which Pati offers her morning prayers; and even the red oxide flooring in Pati's house, which is a rarity these days but was also the flooring in my grandmother's house in Malleshwaram.

Although I never took a road trip with my Paati, I have thoroughly enjoyed bringing to life the quiet, enduring love between Pati, Mommy, and Sejal. Illustrating this book has truly been an emotional journey for me—sweetly satisfying, like a delicious kesari baat!

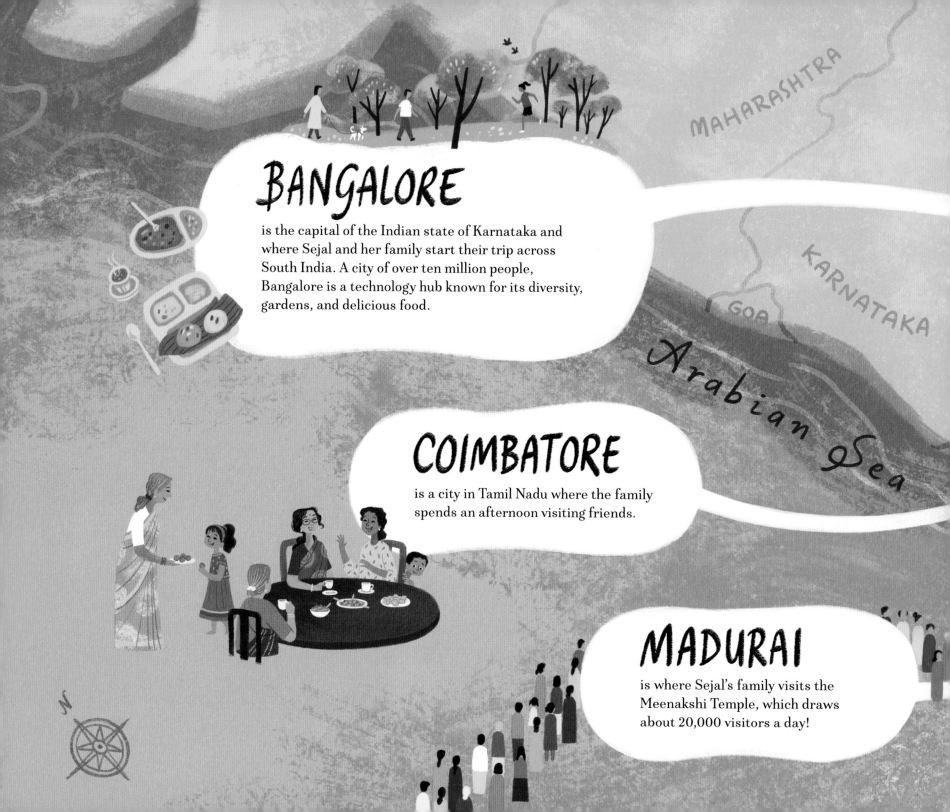

BANGALORE

is the capital of the Indian state of Karnataka and where Sejal and her family start their trip across South India. A city of over ten million people, Bangalore is a technology hub known for its diversity, gardens, and delicious food.

COIMBATORE

is a city in Tamil Nadu where the family spends an afternoon visiting friends.

MADURAI

is where Sejal's family visits the Meenakshi Temple, which draws about 20,000 visitors a day!

MAHARASHTRA

KARNATAKA

GOA

Arabian Sea

ANDHRA PRADESH

CHENNAI

is the capital of the Indian state of Tamil Nadu. This is where Sejal has a dosa that is big enough for her to share with her mother and grandmother!

TAMIL NADU

Bay Of Bengal

KERALA

KANYAKUMARI

is located at the southern tip of India. Known as "Land's End," it is famous for its sunrises and moonrises. It is the place where waters from three oceans meet—the Indian Ocean, the Bay of Bengal, and the Arabian Sea.

Indian Ocean

For my mom and my daughter,
who fill me with joy and strength
—R.L.

To my Paati, who I didn't get to know much,
but who lives on in so many little details
—A.S.

The art for this book was painted digitally.

Cataloging-in-Publication Data has been applied for and may be obtained from the Library of Congress.

ISBN 978-1-4197-4129-6

Text copyright © 2021 Rajani LaRocca
Illustrations copyright © 2021 Archana Sreenivasan
Book design by Heather Kelly

Printed and bound in China
10 9 8 7 6 5 4 3

Abrams Books for Young Readers are available at special discounts when purchased in quantity for
premiums and promotions as well as fundraising or educational use. Special editions can also be created to specification.
For details, contact specialsales@abramsbooks.com or the address below.

Abrams® is a registered trademark of Harry N. Abrams, Inc.

ABRAMS The Art of Books
195 Broadway, New York, NY 10007
abramsbooks.com